A NOTE TO PARENTS

When your children are ready to "step into reading," giving them the right books is as crucial as giving them the right food to eat. **Step into Reading Books** present exciting stories and information reinforced with lively, colorful illustrations that make learning to read fun, satisfying, and worthwhile. They are priced so that acquiring an entire library of them is affordable. And they are beginning readers with a difference—they're written on five levels.

Early Step into Reading Books are designed for brand-new readers, with large type and only one or two lines of very simple text per page. **Step 1 Books** feature the same easy-to-read type as the Early Step into Reading Books, but with more words per page. **Step 2 Books** are both longer and slightly more difficult, while **Step 3 Books** introduce readers to paragraphs and fully developed plot lines. **Step 4 Books** offer exciting nonfiction for the increasingly independent reader.

The grade levels assigned to the five steps—preschool through kindergarten for the Early Books, preschool through grade 1 for Step 1, grades 1 through 3 for Step 2, grades 2 through 3 for Step 3, and grades 2 through 4 for Step 4—are intended only as guides. Some children move through all five steps very rapidly; others climb the steps over a period of several years. Either way, these books will help your child "step into reading" in style!

To my two little polar babies, Hollie and Jill
—S.R.

To Tyler, Peter, David, and Hunter
—L.M.

ISBN 0-439-30922-0

Text copyright © 2000 by Susan Ring.
Illustrations copyright © 2000 by Lisa McCue.
All rights reserved. Published by Scholastic Inc., 555 Broadway,
New York, NY 10012, by arrangement with Random House Children's Books,
a division of Random House, Inc. SCHOLASTIC and associated logos are trademarks
and/or registered trademarks of Scholastic Inc.

12 11 10 9 8 7 6 5 4 3 2   23   5 6 7 8/0

Printed in the U.S.A.

First Scholastic printing, December 2001

STEP INTO READING is a registered trademark of Random House, Inc..

Step into Reading™

POLAR BABIES

by Susan Ring
illustrated by Lisa McCue

A Step 1 Book

SCHOLASTIC INC.
New York Toronto London Auckland Sydney
Mexico City New Delhi Hong Kong

Wake up,
polar babies!
It is a big day.

Polar babies
learn to fish.

This polar baby
loves to fish.

This polar baby
loves to sleep!

Polar babies

learn to swim.

This polar baby
loves to swim.

This polar baby
loves to sleep!

Polar babies learn
to walk on the ice.

This polar baby
loves the ice.

This polar baby
loves to sleep!

Oh, no!

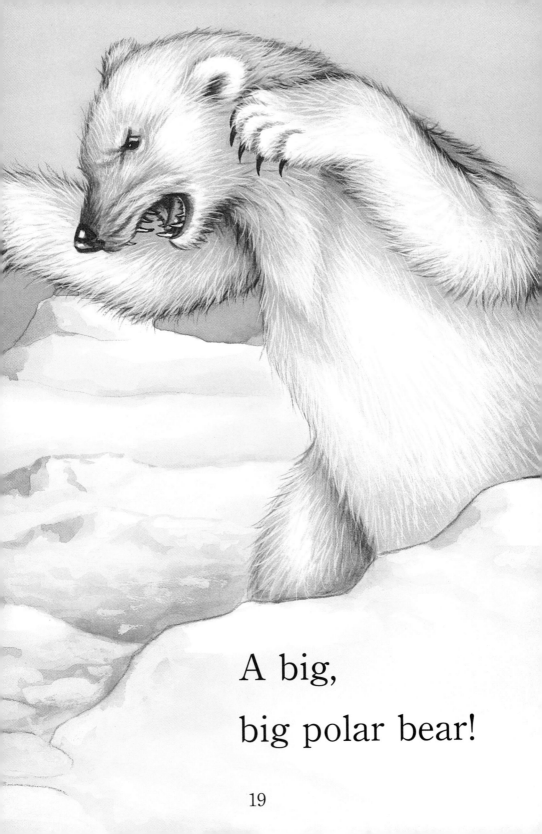

A big,
big polar bear!

Polar babies learn
to run!

Run, polar babies!
Run!

Polar babies run

over the ice…

...past the fishing hole...

...into the water...

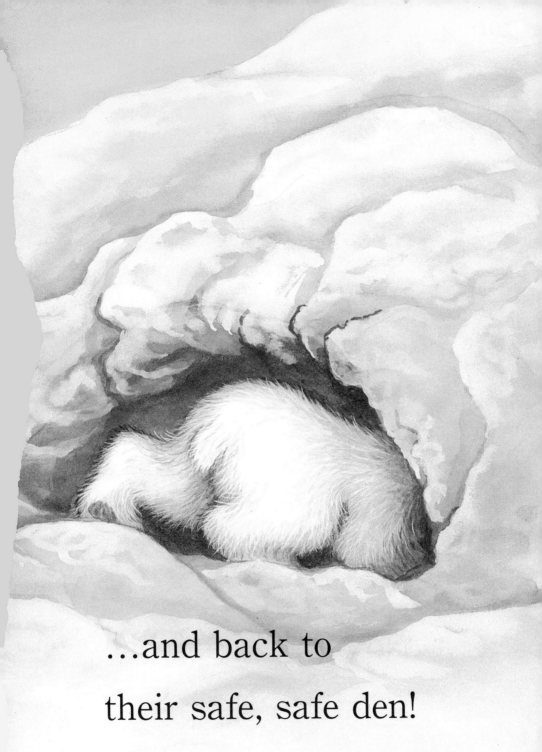

...and back to
their safe, safe den!

Now <u>this</u> polar baby
wants to sleep.

What does this
polar baby want?

Another big day!